The United States

Washington, D.C.

Anne Welsbacher
ABDO & Daughters

visit us at
www.abdopub.com

Published by Abdo & Daughters, 4940 Viking Drive, Suite 622, Edina, Minnesota 55435.
Copyright © 1998 by Abdo Consulting Group, Inc., Pentagon Tower, P.O. Box 36036,
Minneapolis, Minnesota 55435 USA. International copyrights reserved in all countries.
No part of this book may be reproduced in any form without written permission from the
publisher.

Printed in the United States.

Cover and Interior Photo credits: Peter Arnold, Inc., Superstock, Archive

Edited by Lori Kinstad Pupeza
Contributing editor Brooke Henderson
Special thanks to our Checkerboard Kids—Aisha Baker, Priscilla Cáceres, John Hansen,
Stephanie McKenna, Peter Rengstorf, Raymond Sherman

All statistics taken from the 1990 census; The Rand McNally Discovery Atlas of The
United States.

Library of Congress Cataloging-in-Publication Data

Welsbacher, Anne, 1955-
    Washington D.C. / Anne Welsbacher.
    p. cm. -- (United States)
    Includes index.
    Summary: Describes the history, notable sights, people, recreations, and
    occupations of our nation's capital.
    ISBN 1-56239-800-8
    1. Washington (D.C.)--Juvenile literature. [1. Washington (D.C.)]
    I. Title. II. Series: United States (Series)
    F194.3.W45 1998
    975.3--dc21
                                             97-38403
                                           CIP
                                           AC

Contents

Welcome to Washington, D.C. 4

Fast Facts About Washington, D.C. 6

Nature's Treasures 8

Beginnings 10

Happenings 12

Washington, D.C.'s People 18

A Jewel of a City 20

Washington, D.C.'s Land 22

Washington, D.C. at Play 24

Washington, D.C. at Work 26

Fun Facts 28

Glossary 30

Internet Sites 31

Index 32

Welcome to Washington, D.C.

Washington, D.C., is not like any other state. That is because it is not a state! It is a city, but it is called a **district**.

Washington, D.C., is the capital of the United States of America. For this reason, it is called the Nation's Capital. The President and many other people live and work there.

Many people visit every year. They see where our leaders make laws. They see statues and museums. They see cherry trees and pretty parks.

And all Americans see one important thing: their very own city. Washington, D.C., the nation's capital, belongs to us all.

The Capitol in Washington, D.C.

Fast Facts About

WASHINGTON, D.C.

Area/Washington
68 square miles
(177 sq km)
Area/District of Columbia
400 square miles
(1000 sq km)
Population/Washington
626,000 people
Population/District of Columbia
3,400,000 people
City charter
1802
Territorial government
1871
Principal rivers
Anacostia River
Potomac River
Highest Point
Tenleytown;
410 feet (125 meters)
Motto
Justitia omnibus (Justice for all)
Landmarks
Washington Monument, Capitol,
White House, Lincoln Memorial
Famous People
Duke Ellington, Marvin Gaye,
Benjamin Banneker, Connie
Chung

*D*istrict Flag

*A*merican
Beauty Rose

*W*ood Thrush

*S*carlet Oak

Washington, D.C.

The District of Columbia

Detail area

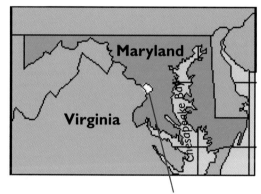

Washington, D.C.

Borders: west (Virginia, Potomac River), north (Maryland), east (Maryland), south (Maryland, Anacostia River)

Nature's Treasures

Washington, D.C., sits on the borders of many rivers. The Potomac runs through the city from the west. The Anacostia runs from the east and meets the Potomac. They empty into Chesapeake Bay, near the Atlantic Ocean.

Many smaller rivers and streams run through the city. Marshes and **swamps** attract many pretty birds and ducks.

Winters are mild and summers are hot and humid in Washington, D.C. Both seasons can be rainy and wet. But spring is pretty. Washington, D.C., is famous for the cherry trees that blossom there in April.

Opposite page: The Potomac River
runs through Washington, D.C.

Beginnings

The first people to live in Washington, D.C., hunted and fished. Later, **Piscataway** people lived there. They were part of the Algonquian nation of people.

In the 1600s, England **claimed** part of the country now called the United States of America. They made their claim into 13 **colonies**.

In 1776, the colonies declared freedom from England. They fought the Revolutionary War, led by General George Washington. The colonies won and became the United States of America.

Now they had to decide where to put the capital. George Washington wanted the capital on a big river so people could carry things on boats to other states. The Potomac River was near both the North and the South. So this area was picked to be the capital.

Buildings were built. The little towns in the area became part of one city. The new capital was named Washington, D.C., after George Washington.

During the 1800s, in Washington, D.C., some African Americans lived in freedom and others were held as slaves. Washingtonians did not think this was right. In 1850, the city outlawed slavery.

In 1861, southern states **seceded** from the United States because they wanted to keep slavery legal. The Civil War was fought. The North won the war in 1865, and slaves were freed. Black men won the right to vote in Washington, D.C. More African Americans moved to the city.

When their city was new, Washingtonians had no voting rights! Later they could vote for some things. But it wasn't until 1964 that they could vote for the president!

The building of the Capitol.

1600s to 1700s

Birth of a Country

1600s: People from England move to the area. Many native **Piscataway** people die from new diseases. Others move away and become part of the nearby Iroquois nation.

1776: The English **colonies** become the United States of America.

1790: The U.S. decides to have a special **district** to be the capital. One year later, George Washington picks the spot. It is in part of Virginia and part of Maryland.

Washington D.C.

1600s to 1700s

Detail area of District of
Columbia

Maryland

1790s to 1800s

Building a Capital

 1790s: Builders begin planning a city with wide streets, pretty views of the nearby woods, and special buildings to honor the importance of the new country.

 1793: A big party celebrates the beginning of work on the Capitol Building, where lawmakers still meet today.

 1814: English soldiers enter the city and burn down many buildings. A thunderstorm puts out the fires and saves some buildings.

Washington D.C.

1790s to 1800s

Detail area of District of
Columbia

Maryland

1840s to 1970s

Freedom for All

1846: The **Smithsonian museum** is built. Later it grows into many museums and a zoo.

1850: Slavery is outlawed in Washington, D.C. In 1865, after the Civil War, it is outlawed in the United States.

1867: Howard University, where many African Americans go to **college**, is opened.

1974: Washingtonians vote for their own mayor for the first time.

Washington D.C.

1840s to 1970s

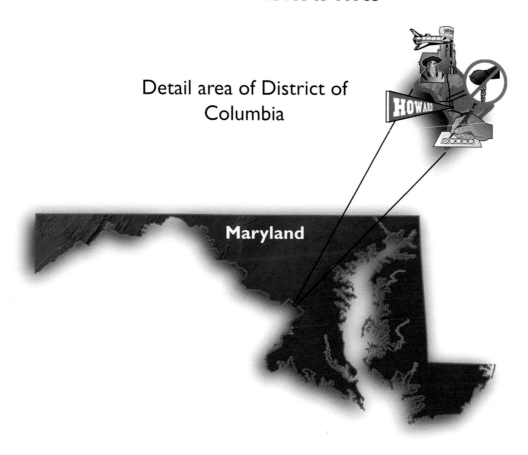

Detail area of District of
Columbia

Maryland

Washington, D.C.'s People

The city of Washington, D.C., has about 600,000 people. But many people live nearby, in Virginia and Maryland. Counting these people, about 4 million people work near the capital.

Duke Ellington was born in Washington, D.C. He led a great jazz band and wrote many jazz songs. Singer Marvin Gaye was from Washington, D.C. John Philip Sousa, who wrote "The Stars and Stripes Forever" and many other marches, was also born in the capital city.

Actors Goldie Hawn, Chita Rivera, and Helen Hayes were born in Washington, D.C. So was Billie Burke, who played Glinda the Good Witch in *The Wizard of Oz*. Famous playwright Edward Albee also is from the capital city.

Benjamin Banneker, a free African American who helped to plan and build the city in the 1700s, was born in Washington, D.C. The famous journalists Connie Chung, Roger Mudd, and Carl Bernstein were born in Washington, D.C.

A famous dad and son team—Benjamin Oliver Davis, Sr. and Jr.—were both from the capital city. Davis, Sr. was the first African American general in the U.S. Army, and his son was the first African American general in the U.S. Air Force.

Benjamin Oliver Davis, Jr.

Billie Burke (left)

Duke Ellington

A Jewel of a City

Washington, D.C., is one of only a few cities in the whole country that was planned before it was built. Its builders thought carefully about where to put everything. So its buildings and streets are very easy to use.

On a map, the city is shaped like a diamond. In the middle is Capitol Hill. This is where many of the country's laws are studied, argued, and made. The Capitol has a famous dome-shaped roof.

The National Mall, a long thin park, stretches out from Capitol Hill. At the other end of the mall are the Lincoln Memorial and the Washington Monument.

Along the mall are many museums and a pretty pool of water. This is where many Americans march for their

rights, visit the city, and see things that remind them of their freedom. Near the mall is the White House, the National Zoo, and Arlington National Cemetery, where many soldiers are buried.

Many neighborhoods were separate towns long ago, but now are part of what is called Washington, D.C. Georgetown has many pretty old houses. Adams-Morgan has people of many different backgrounds—and many kinds of good food to eat!

The National Mall

Washington, D.C.'s Land

The city of Washington, D.C., is 68 square miles (177 sq km). But counting the land around the city, where many more people live, the area is 400 square miles (1,000 sq km).

Much of Washington, D.C., is flat and low. It is near sea level. Rock Creek, in the northwest, is higher, with bluffs and pretty scenery.

Jenkins Hill is one of many small hills in Washington, D.C. This hill has a more famous name. It is Capitol Hill!

The Potomac River once flooded easily. So a pool called the Tidal Basin was built next to it to stop the floods. Many other rivers and streams run from the Potomac through the city.

Japanese cherry blossoms grow near the Tidal Basin. These are the city's most famous plants. In 1912, the

Mayor of Tokyo, in Japan, gave these cherry trees to the city in friendship!

Many other pretty trees grow in the city, too. Some came from other countries and were planted long ago. Others are native to the United States. They include sycamores, red oaks, and willows.

In Washington, D.C.'s parks are wildflowers like skunk cabbages, Virginia bluebells, jack-in-the-pulpits, and bloodroots. Scampering through the parks are gray squirrels, red foxes, muskrats, and flying squirrels. Mourning doves, chickadees, blue jays, and mockingbirds are pretty songbirds that sing to all the people in Washington, D.C.

The Tidal Basin in Washington, D.C.

Washington, D.C. at Play

More than 10 million people visit Washington, D.C., every year! They visit the world's most loved museums, the **Smithsonian museums**. In them they see dinosaurs, paintings and masks, airplanes and spacecraft, the real Star Spangled Banner, and even a rock from the moon!

Visitors also see the Washington Monument, the tallest building in the city, and the Lincoln Memorial, with a giant statue of President Lincoln. They go to the National Zoo and see the only giant pandas in the United States! And they visit the home of the President—the White House.

Visitors and Washingtonians alike enjoy many things in the **district**. They listen to music, see plays, and watch dances at the John F. Kennedy Center for the Arts. They eat at many restaurants that have foods and flavors from all around the world.

Washingtonians play in 150 parks! They hike, ride bikes, and have picnics. And they sail boats in the Potomac River.

Basketball is the **district's** best-loved sport! Kids play it in schools and on the playgrounds. The Georgetown Hoyas have a great college basketball team. The district's professional team is called the Washington Wizards.

The Washington Redskins play football for the district. Another team plays hockey. This team is called the Capitals. Can you guess why?

The National Zoo attracts many visitors.

Washington, D.C. at Work

One in every three Washingtonians works for the United States government. They work for the post office and help make laws. They are janitors, police officers, secretaries, lawyers, and writers.

The next biggest job in the **district** is tourism, helping people who come to visit. Washingtonians work in stores, restaurants, and hotels. They work as tour guides and help people plan their vacations.

Washingtonians also teach and work at many **colleges**. A college is a school you can go to after high school. They help write and print newspapers, magazines, TV shows, radio shows, and films.

And they work in research. They study books, talk to people, and do other things to learn better answers to problems.

The U.S. Supreme Court building in Washington, D.C.

Fun Facts

• The D.C. in the name of the nation's capital stands for "**District** of Columbia." District means it is not part of any other state; it is an area all by itself. Columbia is from the name of Christopher Columbus, who came to North America in 1492.

• The first Miss America was from Washington, D.C. Margaret Gorman received the title in 1921.

• The **Smithsonian Institution** was started with money that a man from England left in his will. James Smithson never even came to the United States. But he wanted to increase and spread knowledge, so he left money for America to start a museum.

• Washington, D.C., is near the Atlantic Ocean, so it almost never snows there. But in 1922, 26 inches (66cm) of snow fell in the district!

•One of the biggest flags ever made was put on display at the Washington Monument in 1981. It was bigger than a football field!

•Because Washington, D.C., is the nation's capital, the **Smithsonian** and many other museums and activities in the **district** are free to all visitors. That is because Washington, D.C., belongs to us all!

The Smithsonian Institute

Glossary

Claim: to take.

Colony: a place that is owned by another country, even if it is far away.

College: a school you can go to after high school.

Constitution: a set of laws written by the people, not a king.

District: an area that is not part of any state.

Manufacture: to make things.

Piscataway: people who lived in Washington, D.C., before the arrival of people from England.

Plantation: a big farm; in the 1600s and 1700s, plantations in the southern U.S. grew cotton and other crops.

Secede: to break away.

Smithsonian Institution: a group of buildings that are all museums; they include the National Air and Space Museum, the National Museum of Natural History, the National Museum of American History, and many more.

Swamp: a muddy, grassy pond.

Internet Sites

The White House for Kids
http://www.whitehouse.gov/WH/kids/html/home.html
Take a look at the White House with your guide Socks the cat.

Washington, D.C. Web
http://www.washweb.net/
This site is very colorful and interactive. See news and current events, top D.C. sites, useful links, and the internet interstate. It also has a browse tool for easy use.

These sites are subject to change. Go to your favorite search engine and type in Washington, D.C. for more sites.

PASS IT ON

Tell Others Something Special About Your State
To educate readers around the country, pass on interesting tips, places to see, history, and little unknown facts about Washington D.C. or the state you live in. We want to hear from you!
To get posted on ABDO & Daughters website, E-mail us at "mystate@abdopub.com"

Index

A

Anacostia 6, 7, 8
Arlington National Cemetery 21
Atlantic Ocean 8

B

Banneker, Benjamin 6, 19

C

Capitol Building 14, 20
Capitol Hill 20, 22
cherry trees 4, 8, 23
Chesapeake Bay 8
Chung, Connie 6, 19
Civil War 11, 16
colleges 26
colonies 10, 12
Columbus, Christopher 28

D

district 4, 12, 24, 25, 26, 29

E

Ellington, Duke 6, 18
England 10, 11, 12, 28

H

Howard University 16

J

Jenkins Hill 22

L

lawmakers 14
Lincoln Memorial 6, 20, 24

M

Maryland 7, 12, 18
museums 4, 16, 20, 24, 29

N

National Mall 20
National Zoo 21, 24
Nation's Capital 4, 28

P

parks 4, 23, 25
Piscataway 10, 12
Potomac River 6, 7, 10, 22, 25
President 4, 11, 24

R

Revolutionary War 10
rivers 6, 8, 22
Rock Creek 22

S

slavery 11, 16
Smithsonian 16, 24, 28, 29
Smithson, James 28

T

Tidal Basin 22

V

Virginia 7, 12, 18, 23

W

Washington, George 10, 12
Washington Monument 6, 20, 24, 29
Washington Redskins 25
White House 6, 21, 24